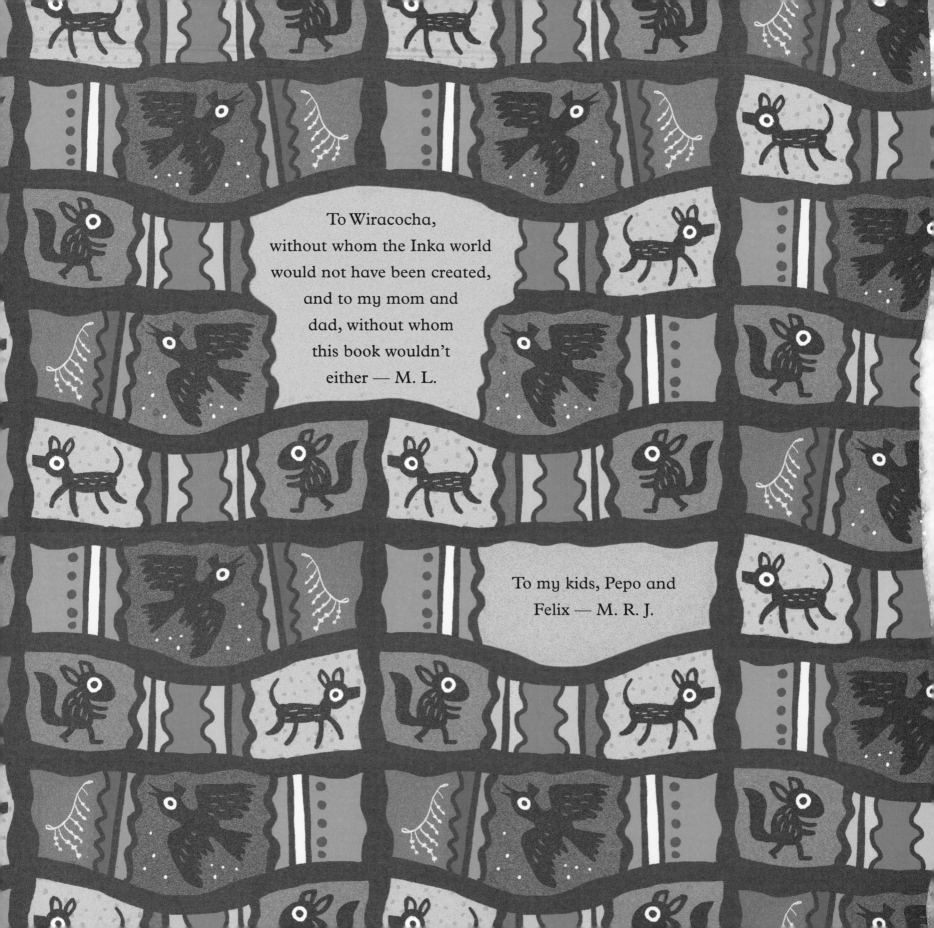

To Wiracocha,
without whom the Inka world
would not have been created,
and to my mom and
dad, without whom
this book wouldn't
either — M. L.

To my kids, Pepo and
Felix — M. R. J.

Run, Little CHASKi!

AN INKA TRAiL ADVENTURE

written by **Mariana Llanos**

illustrated by **Mariana Ruíz Johnson**

Barefoot Books
Step inside a story

Little Chaski wakes up before Tayta Inti shines in the sky. Little Chaski's stomach twists. It is his first day delivering royal messages. Will he be a good messenger?

"Be sure to be strong," says Brave Chaski, his older brother.

"Be sure to be swift," says Big Chaski, his father.

"Be sure to be sharp," says Wise Chaski, his grandfather.

Little Chaski receives his mission from the Qoya, the Queen, herself:

"This khipu is very important. Bring it to the Inka, the King, at the temple before Tayta Inti sets behind those mountains. Do not be late!"

"Yes, great Qoya. I won't disappoint," says Little Chaski, ready to move his legs fast as a puma.

With a ch'uspa full of jerky and kamcha for a snack, and a gleaming white pututu hanging on his side, Little Chaski starts his long journey.

Chakiti, chakiti. His sandals strike the ground as he runs on the Qhapaq Ñan, the Inka Trail, leaving the Qoya's palace behind.

Run, run, Little Chaski, phaway!

But as Little Chaski races, a chinchilla crosses the road and —

Smack!

Kapum!

What a mess!

Little Chaski's knees are sore, but he decides to be strong. Chinchilla looks even worse.

"Are you okay, friend?"

Little Chaski helps Chinchilla and soon he is back on the road.

Oh no! . . . Tayta Inti has tiptoed to the west.

"I must move as fast as a waterfall!" exclaims Little Chaski.

Run, run, Little Chaski, phaway!

But as Little Chaski darts downhill, a wail pierces his ears. It comes from the river —

An allqu is in trouble!
Little Chaski decides to help.

Little Chaski tosses his ch'uspa. Allqu grabs.
With a swift movement, Allqu is back on land!

Allqu shakes. Little Chaski pats her head and then
jumps back on the road.

Oh no! Tayta Inti has slid closer to the west.

"I must run faster than the wind!" exclaims Little Chaski.

Run, run, Little
Chaski, phaway!

But something brushes the bushes and —
it's a condor! He fluffs his feathers. He grunts.

Condor is trapped and scared!

Little Chaski must be sharp. He tosses a rock to distract the bird.

While Condor looks away, Little Chaski rushes to the branch and . . . *zas!* Condor is free!

"Fly away, friend," says Little Chaski as he darts back on the road.

Oh no! Tayta Inti is about to dive behind the mountain!

"I must fly faster than a shooting star!" exclaims Little Chaski.

Run, run, Little Chaski, phaway!

Little Chaski is almost there. *Chakiti, chakiti,* his sandals
slam on the steps. He shoots through the temple doorway just
as Tayta Inti's last rays sink behind the mountains.

Little Chaski takes a minute to catch his breath. Then, he grabs his pututu and blows. Now everyone knows he is there!

"What message have you brought?" asks the Inka.

Little Chaski reaches in his ch'uspa — *chiss, chass.* How could this be? His bag is empty!

The Inka taps his foot. The Reader of the Khipu scowls. *Boom.* Little Chaski's heart pounds!

"Where is the khipu?" demands the frowning Inka.

But just when Little Chaski's cheeks turn red as a huayruro seed, three grateful friends soar from the clouds and —

Swish!

Zoom!

The message falls into Little Chaski's hands!

Little Chaski is relieved, but the Inka wants to know
more. So, Little Chaski tells him the story of how he helped
the animals along the way. The Inka listens and smiles while
the Reader of the Khipu examines the message.

Then the Inka says, "Little Chaski, this was a test for you. You're now an official Chaski of the Tawantinsuyu. On your journey you remembered to be strong, swift and sharp. But you were something even more important: you were kind. And because of your actions, I shall give you your name: Big-Hearted Chaski."

Everyone cheers. And Big-Hearted Chaski's smile glows brighter than Tayta Inti.

Glossary of Quechua words:

* **allqu _(AL-koo)_:**
  a hairless dog found in Peru

* **chaski _(CHAS-key)_:**
  a royal messenger during Inka times

* **chinchilla _(chin-CHEE-yah)_:**
  a rabbit-like animal found in the
  Andes Mountains

* **ch'uspa _(CHOOS-pah)_:**
  a bag used in the Andes region to
  carry coca leaves and other items

* **condor _(KON-dor)_:**
  a vulture found in the Andes
  Mountains that is the largest flying
  bird in the western hemisphere

* **huayruro _(why-ROO-roh)_:**
  a plant native to Peru, with seeds
  that are bright red with a black spot

* **Inka _(EEN-kah)_:**
  the king of the Inka Empire

* **kamcha _(KAM-chah)_:**
  a toasted corn snack

* **khipu _(KEE-poo)_:**
  a recording system made of rope
  and hanging knotted threads

* **phaway! _(PAH-why)_:**
  run!

* **puma _(POO-mah)_:**
  a cat-like animal found in the
  Andes Mountains

* **pututu _(poo-TOO-too)_:**
  a musical instrument made of a
  giant seashell used by chaskis to
  announce their arrival

* **Qhapaq Ñan _(KAH-pak nyahn)_:**
  the Inka Trail, a system of roads

* **Qoya _(KOH-yah)_:**
  queen, wife of the Inka

* **Tayta Inti _(TAI-tah IN-tee)_:**
  father Sun

* **vicuña _(vee-KOON-yah)_:**
  an animal related to llamas and
  alpacas that lives in the Andes

Who were the Inka?

The Inka were a society that ruled the Andes Mountains of South America until after the invasion of the Spanish conquistadors in 1532 CE. Their empire was called Tawantinsuyu, which means Four Regions. Their capital was the city of Cusco. The Inka were skilled builders, engineers and warriors. Their palaces, temples and other developments still impress visitors today.

Drawing of a chaski by Felipe Guaman Poma de Ayala, drawn between 1600 and 1615 CE

Who were the chaskis?

The chaskis were fleet-footed couriers who delivered important messages, news or packages in a relay system throughout the vast territory of the Tawantinsuyu. Boys trained from a young age to be chaskis. They had to be strong, since they ran long distances on difficult roads. Chaskis ran on the Inka Trail, known as Qhapaq Ñan, an advanced system of roads that connected the Tawantinsuyu. If you visit countries in South America, you can still find parts of these roads.

What did the chaskis deliver?

One of the things chaskis delivered was khipus (or quipus). A khipu was a recording device made of a cord and knotted threads of different types. Khipus were used to keep tally and record other important events. Only a few people were able to read the khipus. They were called khipukamayuq and they were specially educated for the job.

COLOMBIA

VENEZUELA

GUYANA

SURINAME

FRENCH GUIANA

ECUADOR

BRAZIL

PERU

BOLIVIA

THE
INKA
EMPIRE
at its largest size
around 1525 CE

CHILE

PARAGUAY

ARGENTINA

URUGUAY

The Inka Empire

The Inka Empire was once the largest civilization in the Americas. The ruler of the Tawantinsuyu was the Inka, believed to be the child of the Sun. Quechua was the official language, but many other languages were spoken across their empire too. The Inka did not have a written language. Machu Picchu, a beautiful ancient city between the Andes Mountains and the Amazon Basin in Peru, is one of the most famous surviving Inka sites.

Inka or Inca?

When Spanish conquistadors invaded the Inka Empire, they used their own language to describe the local people. Spanish spellings of Quechua words became the norm. Today, the languages and thoughts of Indigenous people are recognized. In this book, we use the Quechua spelling Inka, though the Spanish spelling, Inca, is still common.

The Inka Trail

The Inka Trail, or Qhapaq Ñan, was used for official government and military business, and perhaps for religious pilgrimages as well. Two long roads ran north to south along the coast and within the mountains, and various roads connected them. Parts of the Trail included tunnels through mountains and various bridges. The roads also had rest stations along the way.

Animals in South America

Chinchilla

A chinchilla is a rodent from the Andes Mountains with very soft fur and rounded ears.

Allqu

The allqu, a Peruvian hairless dog sometimes believed to have healing powers, has been a popular pet since before the Inka Empire.

Condor

The condor is a vulture, one of the world's biggest flying animals, with a wingspan the size of a small car!

Growing up in Peru, I was always proud of our history — both the Inka Empire and the rich pre-Inka cultures. The Inka accomplished a lot in a fairly short amount of time. Instead of destroying other cultures when they took over lands, they learned from the people they conquered. They built their amazing constructions without wheels or iron tools. I love the way they respected nature and built things that are in harmony with the landscape. I hope readers will be inspired to learn more about the largest empire in the Americas.

— Mariana Llanos

When I was eighteen years old, I explored Bolivia and Peru by bus with two friends. We hiked and camped along the real Inka Trail to reach Machupicchu. I was fascinated by the landscape and culture. I enjoyed diving into Inka culture to create the illustrations for this book. For inspiration, I looked at photographs from my many travels, and Peruvian folk arts like pottery, textiles, wood altars and goldsmithing.

— Mariana Ruiz Johnson

Barefoot Books
Bradford Mill, 23 Bradford Street
West Concord, MA 01742

Barefoot Books
29/30 Fitzroy Square
London, W1T 6LQ

This book was typeset in Amigo and Plantin MT Schoolbook
The illustrations were prepared in
mixed media combined with digital techniques

Text copyright © 2021 by Mariana Llanos
Illustrations copyright © 2021 by Mariana Ruiz Johnson
The moral rights of Mariana Llanos and
Mariana Ruiz Johnson have been asserted

Hardback ISBN 978-1-64686-164-4
Paperback ISBN 978-1-64686-165-1
E-book ISBN 978-1-64686-253-5
Spanish hardback ISBN 978-1-64686-271-9
Spanish paperback ISBN 978-1-64686-217-7

First published in United States of America by Barefoot
Books, Inc and in Great Britain by Barefoot Books, Ltd in 2021
All rights reserved

British Cataloguing-in-Publication Data: a catalogue
record for this book is available from the British Library

Library of Congress Cataloging-in-Publication Data
is available under LCCN 2020951322

Graphic design by Elizabeth Jayasekera, Barefoot Books
Edited and art directed by Kate DePalma, Barefoot Books
Reproduction by Bright Arts, Hong Kong
Printed in China on 100% acid-free paper

1 3 5 7 9 8 6 4 2

Barefoot Books
step inside a story

At Barefoot Books, we celebrate art and story that opens the hearts and minds of children from all walks of life, focusing on themes that encourage independence of spirit, enthusiasm for learning and respect for the world's diversity. The welfare of our children is dependent on the welfare of the planet, so we source paper from sustainably managed forests and constantly strive to reduce our environmental impact. Playful, beautiful and created to last a lifetime, our products combine the best of the present with the best of the past to educate our children as the caretakers of tomorrow.

www.barefootbooks.com

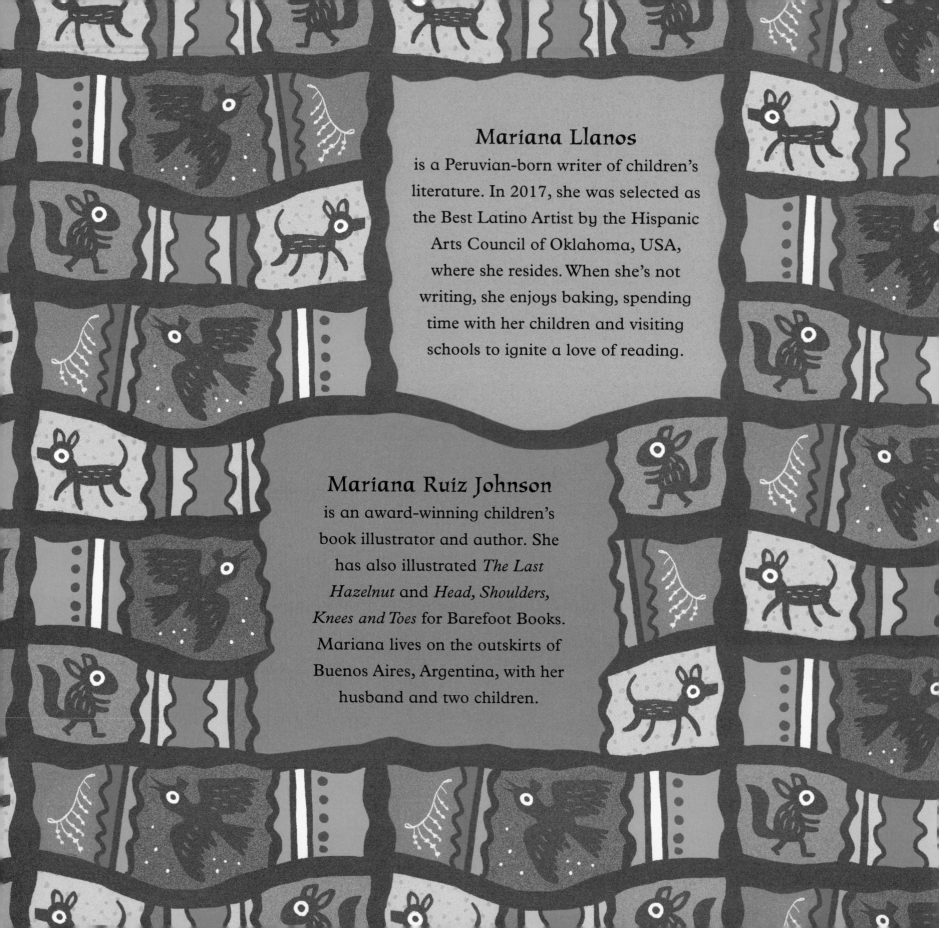

Mariana Llanos

is a Peruvian-born writer of children's literature. In 2017, she was selected as the Best Latino Artist by the Hispanic Arts Council of Oklahoma, USA, where she resides. When she's not writing, she enjoys baking, spending time with her children and visiting schools to ignite a love of reading.

Mariana Ruiz Johnson

is an award-winning children's book illustrator and author. She has also illustrated *The Last Hazelnut* and *Head, Shoulders, Knees and Toes* for Barefoot Books. Mariana lives on the outskirts of Buenos Aires, Argentina, with her husband and two children.